W9-BSV-953

Alligator Boy

Cynthia Rylant & Diane Goode

Harcourt, Inc. Orlando Austin New York San Diego Toronto London www.HarcourtBooks.com

Library of Congress Cataloging-in-Publication Data
Rylant, Cynthia.
Alligator boy/Cynthia Rylant; [illustrated by] Diane Goode.
p. cm.
Summary: A boy puts on an alligator head and tail and is transformed into an alligator boy.
[1. Alligators—Fiction. 2. Stories in rhyme.] I. Goode, Diane, ill. II. Title.
PZ8.3.R96Al 2007
[E]—dc22 2006006049
ISBN 978-0-15-206092-3

H G F E D C B

Printed in Singapore

The illustrations in this book were done in line on paper with watercolor and gouache.
The display and text type was set in Windsor-Light.
Color separations by Bright Arts Ltd., Hong Kong
Printed and bound by Tien Wah Press, Singapore
This book was printed on totally chlorine-free Stora Enso Matte paper.
Production supervision by Jane Van Gelder
Designed by Scott Piehl

For Peter—D. G.

A boy was tired of being a boy.
He hoped to be somebody new.

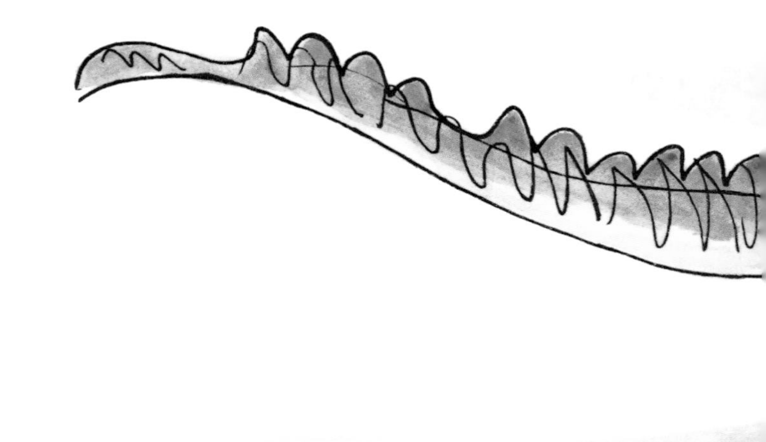

So his auntie who lived in a faraway land
said, "I know just what I should do!"

She sent him a box, a rather big box,

which he opened right then and not later.

He pulled out a head and a very long tail

and became

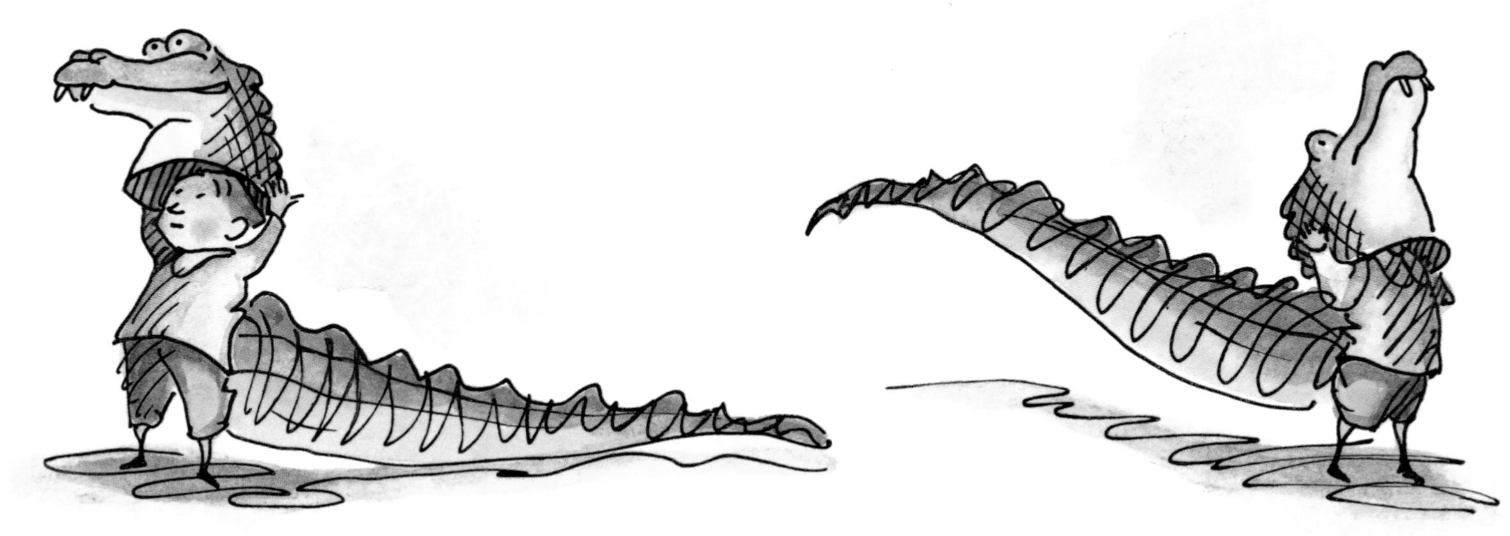

quite a fine alligator.

He found his dear dad and told him the story
of being a lizard, no longer a boy.

"I hope you still like me," the small gator said.
Dad nodded and patted the reptile's green head.

Mother, however, became full of worry.
She put the small lizard to bed in a hurry.

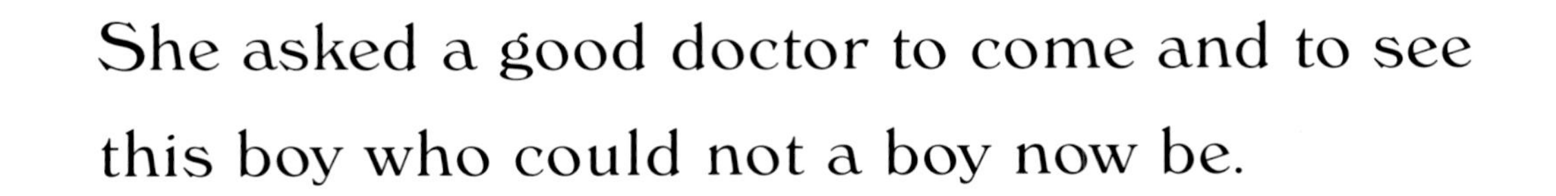

She asked a good doctor to come and to see
this boy who could not a boy now be.

But not having studied green reptiles just yet,

the good doctor said she must call in a vet.

The vet took a look and he said, “It looks well.

Just feed it each day and teach it to spell."

And that's how an alligator got into school.

The vet said he must, that it was the rule.

Once the green lizard got past the school bully,

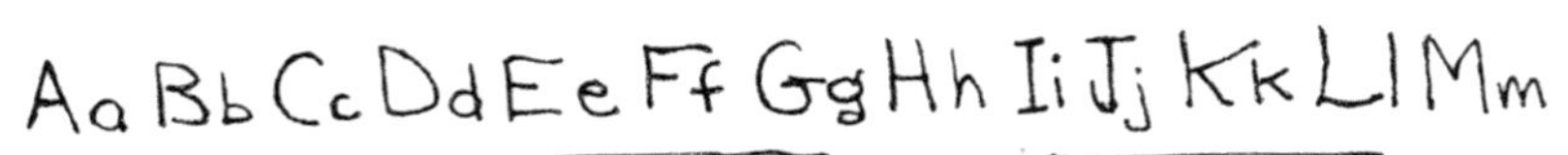

he found he enjoyed the student life fully.

He spelled and he sang from his very long snout.

He cleaned the erasers, he dusted them out.

He saved his small friends with a big, scary roar,

this alligator boy, a boy no more.

His days were quite happy,

his days were a joy....

What a good green life
for an alligator boy.